Grandma Has Wings

By Mary Murray Bosrock

With Alyssa, Isabella, Juliana, Alexandra, Anna, and Lily

Illustrated by Darcy Bell-Myers

BEAVER'S POND
PRESS

ISBN: 978-1-59298-558-6

Library of Congress Control Number: 2012916821
Printed in the United States of America

Edited by Lily Coyle and Kellie Hultgren
Book design by Ryan Scheife, Mayfly Design
Typeset in Univers
First Printing: 2013

17 16 15 14 13   5 4 3 2 1

Beaver's Pond Press, Inc.
7108 Ohms Lane
Edina, MN 55439-2129
(952) 829-8818
www.BeaversPondPress.com

To order, visit www.BeaversPondBooks.com
or call (800) 901-3480. Reseller discounts available.

To my Grandgirls. Thank you for helping me love my wings. —M.M.B.

*

To Grandma Barbara, Grandma Joanie, Grandma Ann,
and Nana Deb. —D.B.M.

Every summer Grandma invites us grandgirls for a sleepover.

After loads of hugs,
we dash upstairs to her closet
and try on all her fancy dresses.

We beg her, "Put on your favorite dress-up dress."

"Oh dear! No, never!" says Grandma.
"That would show my most secret secret!"

A secret?
"Please tell us!"

"Oh, I couldn't."

"We tell you all
our secrets."

Finally Grandma agrees.
"You do share your secrets, so I'll share mine.
Promise you won't tell anyone?"

   "Promise!"
      "We promise!"
         "We pinky promise!"

And so she raises up her squishy, soft arms and says,

Then Grandma puts on her wedding dress.
"This one covers up my big secret."

We sing "Here Comes the Bride"
and surprise Grandpa with our show.

He pretends not
to see the duct tape.

Next, we zip into the kitchen. Grandma says, "Let's make your Great-Grandma Murray's secret brownie recipe."

Another secret!

"These brownies are magic."

Magic brownies?

"The first time Grandpa tasted them, he dropped to one knee and asked me to marry him."

Later at the park, we hop on the swings
and Grandma pushes us.

We hear *flap-flap-flap*
like a bird,

Flap

Flap *Flap*

but there's no bird anywhere.

At the ice cream parlor, Grandma shouts,
"Hi Mr. Tony! I hope you've got enough ice cream
to make us all banana splits with lots of fruit and nuts.

This is my grandgirls' dinner."

While Grandma orders, we whisper about her secret wings.

"Mommy calls Grandma and Grandpa lovebirds."

"Daddy calls Granny a snowbird when she flies south."

"Do Nana's wings carry her to Florida?"

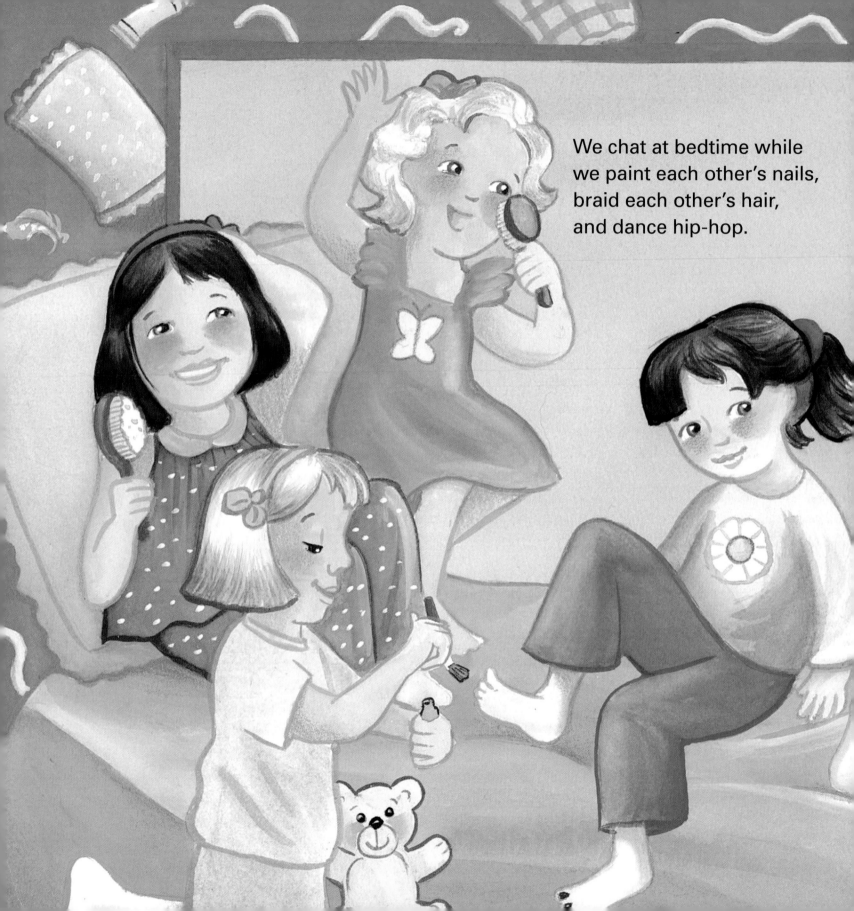

We chat at bedtime while we paint each other's nails, braid each other's hair, and dance hip-hop.

Why do grandmas have wings?

We ask and ask,
until she gathers us around
to tell the story.

"God wanted to create
a special angel to look after
the loveliest of all creation—children.
An angel with lots of time to tell stories.
An angel always ready
to listen to problems.
An angel to praise and adore each child.

God thought and thought,
and then suddenly remembered,
'I don't need a new angel.
I've already got Grandma.
She just needs wings!'"

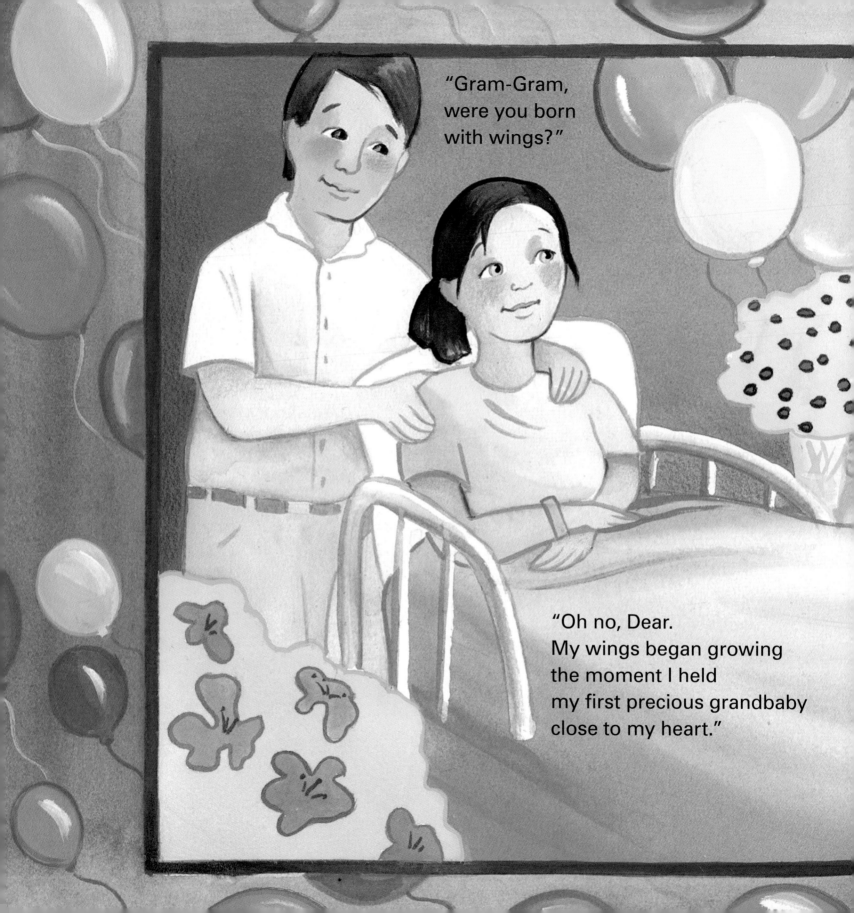

"Granny, will your wings keep growing?"

"Every time I hug one of you, they grow just a wee bit."

"Someday you may not be able to see me.
But when you're tired and troubled
and think you can't go on,

you'll feel my wings
lifting you up."

"When you're afraid to try something hard, you'll feel my wings

giving a gentle nudge from behind."

"When someone breaks your heart
–and someone will–

you'll feel my wings
hugging you
and healing your hurt."

Anytime you see a butterfly
or hear the flapping of birds' wings,

you can close your eyes
and remember,

Grandma's love is forever.

About the Illustrator

Darcy got her wings from a long line of illustrators and artists. Her mom did the technical illustrations for NASA's first lunar lander. Her Great-Grandma Ethel was an oil painter, and her Great-Aunt Jean is a nationally renowned watercolorist. Darcy gets inspiration from her three children, Vanessa, Rowan, and Amelia, and lives with them and her husband, Bruce, in a historic home in Stillwater, Minnesota. When she's not painting, you can find her playing the harp or dancing for fun. Learn about her many other books and awards at www.bellmyers.com.

About the author

Mary Murray Bosrock grew up in Sandusky, Ohio and lives in St. Paul, Minnesota. Mary got her wings when her two sons, Matt and Steve, gave her six granddaughters within eight years. After growing up with six brothers and one sister, Mary was used to boys. She was amazed by these little girls who noticed things like arm fat, brown spots, veins, and dropping chins. She learned to love what she couldn't change by turning it into a story. The grandgirls loved the story so much, Mary decided to share with other grandmas.

GrandmaHasWings.com

Please visit our website to learn
more about the author and the grandgirls.
Share your grandma stories with us, and get
Great-Grandma Murray's secret brownie recipe!